Yahweh

"God's Name Forever"

(Exodus 3:15)

JOE HUEBSCHER

Yahweh
"God's Name Forever"
(Exodus 3:15)

ReadersMagnet, LLC

Contents

W E HAVE A SUPREME BEING, God, who has created all things and who is in charge of all things in His creation. As great as God truly is, and as profound are the truths about Him, we should have no fear or hesitancy about approaching the subject of God and becoming better acquainted with Him. In creating us God greatly wishes to relate to us and have fellowship with us. A brief study of God, especially of Jesus Christ, will yield invaluable truths that can encourage us as Christians, and sustain us in our Christian walk.

The passage in Jeremiah 29:13 expresses what motivates and energizes my quest for God:

"And you shall seek me and find me when you shall seek for me with all your heart" (New King James Version). These words, found in Jeremiah, express what motivates my thoughts and quest for God. I cannot say that I have followed this admonition all of my life, but certainly for most of it. A second passage stated by Jesus in the Sermon on the Mount also expresses my thoughts, "But seek first the Kingdom of God." One more passage that I truly affirm is found in Hebrews, chapter 11: "He who comes to God must believe that He is and that He is a rewarder of those who diligently seek Him" (verse six).

All three passages use the word *seek*. This seeking or searching requires that the person be active in His quest, so much so that "all" his heart is required. In the second passage, Jesus uses the word *first* and in the third, the author of Hebrews uses the word *diligently*. Conclusively, it is the searching out diligently, and the searching first of all before anything else, that will be rewarded by God.

Paul expresses in a different way his desire to know and to seek after God. He says, "that I may know Him" (Philippians 3:10). To know God is different from knowing about Him though the two are related since a person can know much about God, yet not know Him at all. To know Him demands that you meet Him, you talk with Him, and you communicate back and forth. It is then that you are able to form some kind of opinion about Him. But you must know what He thinks and how He thinks. You must experience God's presence in your daily living. The person who experiences God's presence regularly will be rewarded. A person who is not interested or does not show interest by taking great effort will not be rewarded. A person who does not seek will not find. No one finds God by accident. No one just happens to come upon Him. A person finds God by diligently searching for Him.

God has set three conditions for the search. First, a person must believe that God actually exists, "that He is." That is a step that must have already been taken. God has left His imprint on everything He has created so that even the heavens declare the glory of God (Psalm 19:1). A person who has ignored all the evidence and declared himself an atheist has shown himself to possess a closed mind. That person will never see God in anything or in any place.

Second, he must believe that God <u>can</u> be found, that is, that He rewards those searching for Him. The reward must be that they find. A person cannot be passive in the matter; he must have active faith. Our culture today is molded by television, which the vast majority of people watch many hours per day. The result is the formation of a passive society. Citizens live much of their lives projected into the characters on the screen. Active faith trusts God as a person and believes what He says. A person who says, "I believe God" but then steals does not really believe God, for God has said, "You shall not steal" (Exodus 20).

And third, a person must be in earnest; searching "with all his heart." He must seek "first" or "diligently" the Kingdom of God, following the admonition of Jeremiah.

The Person whom you have been seeking, the Creator of the universe——just who is He? And why would I be wanting to seek Him? What does He offer me? The following sections provide the answers to these questions.

God's Name

Frst of all, God's name tells us much about who He is. God has a name, a personal name which is unique and very important to Him even as your name is unique and very important to you. "*Name*" is never plural when it refers to God, and He wants people to know it. He says, "My people shall know my name, And therefore they shall know in that day that I am He who speaks: 'Behold it is I'" (Isaiah 52:6). His name is more than just a descriptive title. In the sentence, "He is a bully," *bully* is only a description. Even to say, "He is the bully" is very little different except to identify an individual as a specific bully. Even so, most of what are called names of God are only descriptions, not names. A name is unique to each individual. Rarely would a person ever find another with the exact same name. My name is Joseph Huebscher, but so is my son's. To make his name unique, he was given an additional name, Lenard. So he is Joseph Lenard and I am Joseph Harold, and we both carry the same third name, Huebscher, which we inherited from my father, Henry. In Matthew 1:21, Joseph was told specifically what name to give the yet unborn Child that Mary was carrying in her womb: "Jesus, for He will save His people from their sins." Jesus then became the name of His incarnation. Christ is a descriptive title that was added when it became known that He was the fulfillment of God's promise.

But more than just a descriptive title, God does have a personal name. And it always occurs in the singular. The third commandment reads, "You shall not take the name of the LORD your God in vain" (Exodus 20:7). This can only refer to God's personal name, the name God gave to Himself and of which He told Moses in the desert in Exodus chapter three. It is spelled with English letters YHWH and translated in most of our English Bibles as LORD in all capital letters. Thus the third commandment says, "You shall not take the name of YHWH God in vain." Again, in Isaiah 42:8 He says, "I am YHWH; that is my name," When translated literally into English, it is "I AM." Few people know that this is God's name even though it occurs in the Old Testament more than 7000 times. The reason for this ignorance is that in our English Bible it always is written the LORD and consequently is not recognized as God's name.

How did God get this personal name? How does anyone get a name? My mother named me. I do not know how you got yours. But always a name is given by someone in authority, usually parents who have authority over their offspring. God named Adam. Whenever God named someone, He chose a name that in some way was fitting to that person. He changed Abram's name to Abraham, meaning "father of many," and Sarai's name to Sarah, meaning "princess." He named the baby of Zechariah and Elizabeth "John," meaning "Yahweh is gracious." But Adam, being the leader, named Eve. Since God gave Adam dominion over the animals, Adam also named them. So how did God get His name? It could only be that He named Himself. So why did He choose YHWH (I AM)? It had to be a name which highlighted His character, a name which is unique to Him, and a name for which only He can fulfill its meaning.

Consider the circumstances around which He told Moses His name in Exodus chapter three. Moses had been reared in Egypt for forty years under the best of conditions. He may even have been trained to be a future pharaoh. But one day while defending an Israelite, he killed an Egyptian and had to flee to the desert to save his own life. He found that his privileged status in Egypt did not guarantee his safety. There he spent another forty years but now under the worst of conditions. As a high class Egyptian, he had learned to despise shepherds, but now he became one. Day after day he led his father-in-law's sheep and goats from one barren valley to another looking for grass. For forty long years he did this. Life was going by and he had to content himself with the prospect of this occupation for his remaining life, and he was already eighty years old.

In this situation God met him in a spectacular way. He spoke to him from a burning bush and informed Him that His name was YHWH. He chose a method whereby Moses could not mistake His voice for something else. Moses must have thought that God was nowhere near the place where he was. Then he saw the burning bush, which immediately got his attention. Then when God spoke to Moses out of the bush, Moses' attention was even greater than before. God was even there in that forsaken place, and Moses was not forgotten. To emphasize His presence in these barren hills, God told Moses to remove his sandals because this place was holy. The I AM was there. I AM met him in a place he thought no one would ever find him. Moses could not escape God. One aspect of God's uniqueness, then, is His "I AMness," His transcendence. There is no place where He, that is I AM, is not. He transcends all space.

But above all else, this name emphasizes God's existence. The philosopher Descartes said, "I think, therefore I am." Thinking proved his existence. With God, His existence is explicitly stated in His name. Since we do not detect Him with our senses in everyday life, it is very easy to ignore Him, then forget Him, and then deny Him. Above everything else, God exists. The focal point of all history points this out as we use the terms A.D. and B.C. As a child, I was told that no one could prove that there is a God. Now, I know that there is no need of proof because God Himself has proven His existence. He predicted that He would die by crucifixion and that after three days He would be resurrected. Isn't it a profound proof of His existence that what He predicted did in fact occur? There is ample proof that the Jesus of the Bible was an actual historical person. There is also ample evidence that He predicted His death numerous times before He made that final trip to Jerusalem. Not only did He predict His death along with numerous other predictions of it from the Old Testament prophets, but He also gave numerous details describing it and always mentioning His resurrection three days later. Then three days following His crucifixion He actually fulfilled this prediction.

When He did arise, He made sure He was seen both by different people and different numbers of people at various times and places. Neither could His enemies produce His dead body though it had been carefully guarded. Finally, the existence of the church more than two thousand years later, after numerous attempts by those who refused His grace and forgiveness to end its existence, attest to the fact that we have a living Christ. He is truly I AM, the supernatural God.

This name not only merely implies existence, but it also implies existence as a person, one having both self-awareness and self-determination. The name contains the first person personal pronoun. Though He is not human except through the incarnation, He certainly has personality. He also knows Himself perfectly and possesses perfect self-determination. A human can only plan his actions subject to circumstances or cancellation, but God can determine His plans absolutely with no regard to circumstances.

His name also implies an eternal existence. God expands all time. His name is not "I Was." God is outside of time. He has no beginning and no end. Jesus claimed this name for Himself in the context of time in the Book of John when He stated that "before Abraham was, I AM" (John 8:58). He further says in Revelation 1:8, "I am the Alpha and the Omega, the Beginning and the End,...who is and who was and who is to come." Here are mentioned all three periods of time, past, present, and future, following the words "I am." The same is true of Revelation 16:5, "The One who is and who was and who is to be." This sets Him apart from His image, man, who as a created being by necessity had a beginning.

Furthermore, His name implies His independence. He does not need anything from us to exist or even to meet His own necessities or wishes. He exists apart from any portion of His creation. He is the Uncaused Cause.

Finally, His name implies immutability. He is always the same; He never changes. Should He ever change, He would not be exactly the same person as He was formerly. But He cannot change, for He is God, the Unchangeable One.

Jesus And Yahweh

WHEN JESUS WALKED ON THIS earth, He was asked about His Father, God, AND SPECIFICALLY WHO God is. Jesus' response was this: "He who has seen me has seen the Father." We learn about God through the Person of Jesus, the One who was sent to this earth to redeem us from our sins. Jesus was God incarnate, the God-man, the Person who infused history with His presence. Jesus is the "I AM" of the New Testament.

In the Greek language of the New Testament the name becomes two words, *ego eimi* emphasizing the "I" when just one word, *eimi*, would be both usual and sufficient. Jesus uses the one word *eimi* in John 13:13, where it is obvious that He is not referring to Himself as deity. But in the instances where He uses the two words, *ego eimi*, with no nominative following, I am convinced He is referring to His name YHWH. The fourteen instances in the Gospels are these: Matthew 24:5 (Mark 13:6 and Luke 21:8 refer to the same instance); Mark

14:62; Luke 22:70. The following passages are all in John's Gospel (4:26.6:20; 8:24, 28, 58; 13:19; 18:5, 8) except the last, Matthew 28:20. This last one may be questionable since it is followed with a prepositional phrase, "with you." However, previous to this He claims "all authority in heaven and earth" followed by a demand to make disciples. Clearly, He is addressing them as their God, I AM.

Not only is Jesus using His name of deity in the above references, but each one in its own setting is emphasizing a different aspect of the name's meaning. For example, **Luke 21:8** occurs in a prophetic context where Jesus predicts that many will claim to be I AM in the future and His followers are not to be deceived.

In **John 4:26,** a different context, Jesus is speaking with the Samaritan woman. She understands that Jesus must be a prophet and that some time in the future the Messiah will come, who will appear as a great teacher instructing them in all things. Jesus responded by saying, "I AM." This is the one time that He admitted to being the Messiah or the Christ other than to His disciples. But her understanding of the Messiah was that He was to be a great teacher, not the great warrior which the Jews were expecting. Jesus used His name, I AM, to equate the great teacher with God and Himself and her concept of Messiah.

Still another setting or context is seen in a boat on the Sea of Galilee. It was in the middle of the night on the evening following the feeding of the five thousand when a fierce wind arose. The disciples became frightened. Then Jesus came to them walking on the water. As He approached, He called out His name, "I AM, do not be afraid." He then got into the boat with them, and immediately they were at their destination. As YHWH, He had authority over both the wind and the water, which He had created. That day His disciples had witnessed three supernatural events: the multiplication of the small loaves and two small fish to be sufficient to satisfy the hunger of possibly as many as ten thousand people since only the men had been counted; Jesus walking on the water; and reaching their destination immediately. They had had sufficient food for their bodies earlier in the day, and now they had an abundance of food for their thoughts as they contemplated who their teacher actually was in light of the day's events. Jesus clearly was teaching them that He was the I AM or YHWH, who was far superior to His creation.

John, chapter eight, finds Jesus in a discussion with the Pharisees, the conservative party in Israel. They accuse Him of being a liar (8:13). He rebukes this accusation by pointing out His relationship to the Father. Using His name of deity, I AM, in verse eighteen, He bears witness of Himself and then also adds the testimony of the Father. Then to these people He says that they will die in their sins if they do not believe that I AM (8:24). Faith in Him as YHWH was necessary for forgiveness. Further, to these same people He said, "When you lift up the Son of Man, then you will know that I AM" (8:28). The events accompanying the crucifixion clearly showed His identity: the sky was darkened, the veil in the temple separating the Holy Place from the Most Holy Place was torn in two from top to bottom, an earthquake occurred, and His body was missing in spite of a guard having been placed at the tomb. Even the Roman centurion in charge of the crucifixion confessed, "Truly this was the Son of God." This chapter in John ends by Jesus calling them, the Pharisees, liars (8:55). Since they were the conservative party in Israel who boasted much of having Abraham as their Father, Jesus mentions how Abraham rejoiced to meet Him as he had done just before the destruction of the cities of Sodom and Gomorrah. The Pharisees sneered, "You're not even fifty years old." To this challenge Jesus responded, "Before Abraham was, I AM." Because of this statement the Pharisees sought to stone Him for blasphemy since He had identified Himself as YHWH, transcending all time.

The setting for **John 13:19** is the evening before the crucifixion. Jesus had just washed His disciples' feet, and then He predicted His betrayal and who would accomplish it. His ability to know the hearts and secret plans of those so close to Him and one another must have greatly shaken them for they "looked at one another perplexed." He made this prediction to confirm their belief that He was really I AM.

The last occurrence in **John's Gospel, 18:5 & 8,** came only hours later in the Garden of Gethsemane. Judas came to the garden with some troops to arrest Him. Jesus stepped forward and asked who they were looking for (18:4). They responded, "Jesus of Nazareth." He replied, "I AM," at which they drew back and fell to the ground, (18:6). Jesus then repeated His question in verse eight. All the power and authority of men and the armies that they might muster would have no effect on Him unless He permitted such a circumstance to occur.

I must mention two additional times which do not occur in John's Gospel but do in the other three Gospels. After Jesus was arrested, He was taken to Annas and from there to the Sanhedrin. There the high priest, Caiaphas, put Him under oath (Matthew 26:63) and then demanded He tell exactly who He was. Was He the Christ, the Son of God? Jesus answered by saying "I AM" **(Mark 14:62)** and then referred to Himself as the Son of Man, a title He frequently used of Himself, taken from Daniel 7:13 & 14, and which is clearly a title of deity. The high priest understood this claim of deity since he then accused Jesus of blasphemy and deserving of death. Thus, Jesus was officially put to death by the Jews for claiming His name of deity, I AM or YHWH. Caiaphas then tore his garment and pronounced the death sentence.

The final occasion was just before His ascension and is found in **Matthew 28:18-20.** The I AM is immediately followed by a prepositional phrase. He announces to His disciples that He has "all authority." This assertion clearly puts Him in the role of deity as no other statement would have done. This announcement is then followed with an order, "Go and make disciples," which in turn is followed with a promise, "lo, I AM with you" even to the end of the age.

Each of these instances where Jesus claimed to be I AM emphasizes a different aspect of His person. In John four He is the teaching Messiah; in chapter six He is in charge of the various forces of nature; in chapter eight He relates to nonbelievers; in chapter thirteen to His disciples; in chapter eighteen to forces of power on planet earth; finally, in Mark to the government officials of His own country. I also will mention the one reference in Matthew where, as the King of kings, He addresses His subjects.

This name does precisely what a name is supposed to do. It not only identifies God, but at the same time it points out that which is unique about Him: unique in His relationship to His image which He is creating as well as His entire creation. Since mankind is in His image, made in His likeness, it only follows that mankind has many, if not most, of His attributes in some limited fashion. It is also the name He is very careful to guard. He says in Isaiah 42:8, "I am Yahweh, that is my name; and my glory I will not give to another." Again, in Exodus 20:7, He says, "You shall not take the name of Yahweh your God in vain, for Yahweh will not hold him guiltless who takes His name in vain."

I Am With A Predicate

NOT ONLY DID JESUS CLEARLY define Himself as I AM in the selected passages that have already been discussed, but He used the "I AM" with the predicate in a number of instances. Particularly are these instances seen in John's Gospel. This is reasonable since John wrote so that people would "believe that Jesus is the Christ, the Son of God, and that believing you may have life in His name" (John 20:31). These instances number seven and point to His deity as only God could be what each states.

In John 6:35 He says, **"I AM the bread of life."** This saying follows the miracle of the feeding of the five thousand. In the evening, Jesus and His disciples had gone to Capernaum and when the people finally found Him, they requested a sign even though He had miraculously fed them the day before. He told them not to labor for physical food but for the food that "endures to everlasting life" (6:27). Moses gave only physical food, but the real food which can satisfy that intense spiritual hunger God keeps on supplying in the person of Jesus, who is the bread of life. In their culture bread was the principal part of every meal, even as "meat and potatoes" were of mine while I was a child in northern Wisconsin. Jesus is the real food, the only food which can satisfy our spiritual hunger.

"I AM the Light of the world" (John 8:12). The main quality of light is that it illuminates. To the mind it is what enables a person to comprehend, to understand. To have good knowledge of a thing, a person must have some understanding of its origin and purpose. Since He created all things (John 1:3), He determines its purpose, which is mainly an environment for His image. Furthermore, He has given to us an instruction manual telling us our purpose, "to be conformed to the image of His Son" (Romans 8:29) in the environment in which He has placed us. He enlightens us every step of the way. It is only in the light of Him that we can know about ourselves. The big questions, Who am I? Where did I come from? What am I doing here? Where am I going? And What am I worth? are all answered in the light from Him. Christianity is based on faith in a real historical person, whereas other worldviews, also based on faith, must rely upon false premises and concepts.

"I AM the Good Shepherd" (John 10:14). No doubt the Lord had Ezekiel 34 in mind as He spoke these words. This entire chapter addresses shepherds and sheep. The first ten verses mention evil shepherds who do not care for God's sheep, but in verse eleven God says, "I myself will search for my sheep and seek them out." Verse 23 adds, "I will establish one shepherd over them and He shall feed them––My servant David. He shall feed them and be their shepherd." Jesus now fulfills this passage as a direct descendant of David. He further states that the Good Shepherd "lays down His life for the sheep." This is going to the extreme. An average, normal shepherd may attempt to protect his flock but is never expected to put his life on the line. Jesus gave His life for His sheep.

"I AM the Door" (John 10:7 and 9). The shepherds of Israel would lead their sheep into an enclosure at night for protection. This enclosure or sheepfold had only one door. Several shepherds might keep their sheep in the same fold, but only shepherds could go in with their sheep. Jesus claims that He is the door and anyone entering "will be saved and go in and out and find pasture" (verse 9). There is only one door for all mankind so that salvation can be entered only through Jesus Christ.

"I AM the resurrection and the life" (John 11:25). This saying was spoken to Martha just before Jesus would bring Lazarus back to life. It occurred only a short time before His own death and resurrection. The two, Lazarus coming back to life and Jesus coming back to life, are different in nature since Lazarus died again at some time in the future while Jesus did not. When Lazarus came out of the tomb, he had a mortal body and would die again, whereas Jesus, when He came out of the tomb, had an immortal one and would never again face physical death. Jesus' purpose for visiting Lazarus' tomb seems more to demonstrate who He is than to show sympathy for the family. He could not have wept out of sorrow, knowing that He was about to bring Lazarus back to life. It seems to be rather from a feeling of disgust or sadness because of their doubts about who He really was. He then brought Lazarus back to life after he had been dead four days. Some day He would resurrect Lazarus. But He was more than the facilitator of returning Lazarus back to life. He is the resurrection and the life. At birth we each receive life from our parents, each parent contributing 24 chromosomes, whereas at the new birth we each receive life from Him who said, "I am the resurrection and the life." In John 10:27-28, He says, 'My sheep hear my voice and I know them and they follow me. And

I give to them eternal life and they shall never perish; neither shall anyone snatch them out of my hand."

"I AM the Way, the Truth, and the Life" (John 14:6). Each of the three nouns has an article. This marks off an exclusiveness, particularly with the word *way*. He does not show them the way for He is the Way, the only way to the Father, the way to God. It is only through His death that sinners can approach God.

Regarding the truth, Westcott comments that as used here, the word sums up "all that is eternal and absolute in the changing phenomena of finite being." Truth is not just about God, but rather it is God revealing Himself in Jesus. With this saying, Jesus is claiming an exclusive position.

"I AM the True Vine" (John 15) The presence of the word *true* implies a contrast with a false. The Old Testament uses this analogy in Psalm 80, Jeremiah 2, and Ezekiel 15. In each instance God is rebuking the Israelites for their sin because they failed to produce fruit. What constitutes fruit is not mentioned in any of these passages. Since God's purpose for the whole universe is to make an image of Himself, fruit probably refers to godly characteristics such as those found in Galatians 5:22: "But the fruit of the Spirit is love, joy, peace, longsuffering, kindness, goodness, faithfulness." Two necessary requirements must be met if a branch is to bear fruit. The first mentioned is cleanliness, while the second is abiding in Him. Both require the Holy Spirit which He, Jesus, will give shortly after He departs to return to the Father (chapter 16). Since He put the abiding as an imperative, the believer must assume that responsibility. There are so many distractions in every day living that getting our minds and motives sidetracked becomes natural. The main point that Jesus is stressing is that fruitful lives must continually maintain contact with the source of life, Himself.

Using The Third Person In His Name

G OD IS REFERRED TO AND understood as the "I AM" of scripture. Jesus is God and therefore the "I AM," particularly seen in the New Testament passages. We learn about God through the discussion of His name and through the Person of Jesus Christ.

Jesus could readily use the first person personal pronoun in His name, I AM. When anyone else refers to His name, it seems more natural to use the third person as He Is or God Is. There are four instances in the New Testament where "GOD IS" is followed by a predicate nominative. These four instances show something very basic about the nature of God and His relationship to man. They inform us as to how a relationship with Him is possible, how universal is His availability, what motivates God toward a relationship, and the consequences of rejecting a relationship.

The first instance occurred when Jesus was speaking to the Samaritan woman in John chapter four. She inquired about where the proper place to worship might be, whether in Mt. Gerizim, where the Samaritans had an altar, or in Jerusalem, where the Jews worshipped. Jesus replied that the Jews had the proper place but that in the future, the place of worship would make no difference. The reason that He gives is that **"GOD IS SPIRIT."** "Spirit" is in contrast to any physical properties. God has no physical body except in the body of Jesus in the incarnation. Since God is not physical, worship is not primarily physical but spiritual. A physical place to worship for everyone in the world becomes irrelevant or even nonsense because the spirit of God transcends all space. This also explains why God cannot be either seen or touched and leaves an open question to many as to whether He even exists. Because He is spirit, it is possible for God to relate to every individual and be worshiped in either Jerusalem or Mt. Gerizim or both at the same time or any other place as well. As spirit He is not limited by either space or time.

The Apostle John in his first epistle says, **"God is light."** He immediately adds that "in Him is no darkness at all. If we walk in the light. . . ." (I John 1:5,7). We are implicitly led to believe that physical darkness is not in his mind but rather he is speaking about the way a person lives. Since this universe was created by God in its entirety and is now equally sustained by Him, He knows the best way for us to live. This He is willing to communicate, to illuminate or enlighten. Understanding God, His character, and His ways and consequently living accordingly is the best possible way to spend our time here on God's earth. Especially important for estranged men is to find their way back to God. For this, God gives an abundance of light.

To say that God is light is not much different from saying that God is truth. Our minds are illuminated by truth. It affects every area of our lives. Physical light is one component that is absolutely necessary for life, every kind of life. So mental light is necessary for any kind of meaningful human life. To know where we are from, why we are here, what we are to be doing, and where we will eventually end up gives meaning to life. To believe in no God but rather that the universe came about, and consequently us, by time and chance is to have no truth. Truly, God is light.

The apostle John is also the one who wrote **"God is love"** (I John 4:8). God's existence is not centered on Himself. He is not a consumer. Unlike humans, He is not continually looking out for number one, Himself. He is always giving. He is like the widow's vessel of oil that would not run dry until all the vessels she and her son had borrowed were full (II Kings 4:1-7). He gives out of His fullness from which we all have received. *Agape* love is not so much a feeling as it is an innate characteristic, always there, always giving the very best, always giving oneself. That is our God. He never has a selfish thought or motive as He gives Himself freely for our good.

We should never think of God's wanting "glory" as being selfish. I rather think of it as a means of loving us. If we do not put God in a place of glory, we would put ourselves there and consequently function as our own god. We would then treat God as our servant. It is true that our Lord came "not to be ministered unto but to minister," to serve. But that does not mean that we should treat Him as our servant since we are not His boss. His servant attitude comes from within. He also taught His disciples to think of themselves as "unprofitable slaves." He never called them that, but He told them to think of themselves as such. We have only one King and it certainly is not to be ourselves. Jesus is our King, and He became incarnate so that He could minister or serve because He is love and as love He is always giving.

The fourth instance occurs in Hebrews 12:28, **"For our God is a consuming fire."** The author of Hebrews takes this label from several passages in the Old Testament, specifically Exodus 32:10. Deuteronomy 4:24, and Deuteronomy 9:3. The first was given when Moses descended from Mt. Sinai and found the Israelites worshiping the golden calf. Deuteronomy 4:24 adds that God is a jealous God. This verse issues a warning lest they forget their covenant with God. The second promises God's protection against the descendants of Anak. God will go before them as they enter and will destroy the present inhabitants.

The author of Hebrews directs his statement to Christians, to those who are His children. As gratitude to God for what is promised to them in the future, a kingdom which cannot be shaken, they need to offer to God acceptable worship, mindful that He is a consuming fire.

Chapter twelve of Hebrews informs us that God is not indifferent to the circumstances we as His children are going through. The people to whom this book was written were going through severe persecution, but as yet they had not shed any blood (verse four).

The author tells them that they are in a race (verse one) but were to keep their eyes on Jesus (verse two). He too, had gone through severe pain, verse three. Besides, the difficulty they were having was God's chastening (verses seven through eleven) and in the end would yield the "peaceable fruit of righteousness." They were not to become discouraged but were to look carefully out for one another (verses twelve through seventeen). The "grace of God" is always conscious of living under the guidance and provision of God. "Bitterness" comes when a person thinks that life is not fair. This attitude is contagious and affects "many." It comes when we look too much at our own circumstances and become dissatisfied.

In verse twenty-two the author tells them to consider what is in store for us. We have a future. We are receiving a kingdom which cannot be shaken (verse twenty eight). "Grace" in verse twenty nine has the idea of being thankful. We are to serve God with a thankful attitude with reverence and a godly awe. And then comes verse twenty-nine, "For our God is a consuming fire."

This is not in a context of God's dealings with the ungodly people who reject Him. These are His own people. He is going to perform a shaking, that is, a removal of all those things which do not meet His approval. Therefore, we as Christians need a "godly fear," for we are the ones who will be shaken, that is, who will have removed from us all those things of which God disapproves.

The writer of Hebrews says that we are not standing at the foot of Mt. Horeb as the Israelites were when God gave to Moses the Ten Commandments and terrified them with darkness and the sound of a trumpet. They had the threat of immediate death, but we have come to the heavenly Jerusalem. However, if they did not escape, how shall we escape if we "turn Him away." "God is a consuming fire who will destroy all that is within us of which He disapproves and which does not fit His purpose.

But how can this be harmonized with "God is love" as well as "how can a God of love send anyone to hell"? To answer the first, "How can a God of love be a consuming fire to a Christian?" we must consider the nature of love. Because He is a God of love, He is determined to give only the very best. On the flip side, He must eradicate all that is inferior in His children if they are to be like Christ. Rejection of God's purpose for our life and what He deems best cannot co-exist throughout eternity. It appears that sometimes this eradicating process will be quite painful for we must all appear before the judgment seat of Christ that everyone may receive a reward for the things done while living in the body "whether good or bad" (II Corinthians 5:10). The book of Colossians adds, "Knowing that from the Lord you will receive the reward of the inheritance; for you serve the Lord Christ. But he who does wrong will be repaid for what he has done, and there is no partiality" (Colossians 3:24-25).

The Fear Of God

G OD AS A "CONSUMING FIRE" brings to mind a related phrase "the fear of God." This phrase is very common in the Bible. It occurs at least 217 times in both the Old and New Testaments, in addition to 43 times with the words "feared," "fears," and "fearing." It also occurs numerous times expressed in other words altogether. One example is found in Genesis 3:8. Both Adam and Eve had eaten of the forbidden fruit when God came to visit. The serpent had told Eve that God had lied when He told them that they would "surely die" if and when they ate of that fruit, and thus there would be no death and hence no accountability. Eve could therefore be like God in deciding for herself what was good and what was evil. She liked the idea of no accountability and therefore could decide for herself. She ate the fruit and also gave some to Adam, who ate as well. When God came, they both hid for they had disobeyed and now must give account. They now feared God.

In our Christian culture today, the fear of God is mostly neglected or explained in such a way that it may even mean the opposite, as "awe" or even "esteem." Yet I am convinced that the phrase almost always carries the concept of accountability. I once questioned a person regarding a lie she had told to me. She explained, "Oh, God will forgive me," showing no remorse whatsoever. I call this "cheap grace."

The first time the "the fear of God" occurs in the Bible is in Genesis 20:11. Here Abraham had lied to Abimelech regarding Sarah being his wife, so God had to intervene to protect her. When Abimelech questioned Abraham about his lie, Abraham responded, "Because I thought surely the fear of God is not in this place; and they will kill me on account of my wife. . . ." The fear of God, that is, the thought of answering to God and "surely dying," would have kept Eve from eating the forbidden fruit; and the fear of God, that is, the people of that place being fully aware that they had to give an account to God for their treatment of Sarah, would have kept Abimelech from taking Sarah and Abraham needing to lie regarding her.

The Lord clearly taught the Israelites to fear Him at the time He gave them the law. He told Moses, "You shall set bounds for the people all around, saying, 'Take heed to yourselves that you do not go up to the mountain or touch its base. Whoever touches the mountain shall surely be put to death'" (Exodus 19:12). "Now Mount Sinai was completely in smoke, because the LORD descended upon it in fire. Its smoke ascended like the smoke of a furnace, and the whole mountain quaked greatly" (Exodus 20:18). In verse twenty, Moses explained to the people why God went to such lengths to create fear, "so that you may not sin." God specifically taught His people to fear Him: "I will let them hear my words, that they may learn to fear Me all the days they live on the earth, and that they may teach their children."

As Jesus is YHWH and as He is **life,** when Adam and Eve sinned, they were immediately separated from life; that is, they immediately died. It was the natural consequence of disobedience. Adam continued to exist on planet earth until he was 930 years old before his body died, but now it was in a fallen state. All his offspring were born in a fallen state, that is, spiritually dead. Whether he and Eve continued to be separated from God, we do not know. When God questioned him as to whether he had eaten of the forbidden fruit, he answered God accurately. "The woman whom You gave to be with me, she gave me of the tree, and I ate" (Genesis 3:12). Was this a true confession or was he simply blaming Eve and/or God? I do not know.

In the New Testament, Jesus taught His disciples to "fear God." In Matthew 10:28 He says to them, "And do not fear those who kill the body but cannot kill the soul. But rather fear him who is able to destroy both soul and body in hell." He then immediately explains how much the Father cares for them, much more than He cares for sparrows, so they need not live in terror.

In Acts, chapter five, occurs a vivid example of God teaching the early church to fear. In the account of Ananias and Sapphira his wife, they both lied and they both died publicly. The result was fear, as related in Acts 5:11 "Great fear came upon all the church and upon all who heard these things," God's desire to teach the early church to fear had to be the motive for God bringing about their death.

In Romans, chapter three, Paul summarizes the state of the human race when he quotes from Psalm fourteen and fifty-three and then concludes with this statement from Psalm thirty-six: "There is no fear of God before their eyes." This seems to be the reason for all of the above. There is no sense of accountability. This is the indictment of our generation.

Accountability is not in the minds of most Christians. They do not know how to harmonize it with the grace of God. If Jesus died for my sins, then they have all been forgiven, past sins, present sins, and future sins, when I came to the cross. Never will they be brought up again. Romans 8:1 assures us that "there is now, therefore, no condemnation to those who are in Christ Jesus." This is true, but the subject deserves greater attention, which I will give it later.

The Purpose Of God

THE FIRST CHAPTER OF THE Bible, Genesis chapter one, sets forth the six days of creation, culminating in the creation of man in the image of God. This last item is God's crowning work and seems to be the purpose for all the others. This is confirmed by Paul in Romans, chapter eight. In Romans 8:28, 29 he says, "And we know that all things work together for good to those who love God, to those who are the called according to His purpose." Chapter one of Genesis lists six things before He creates man and calls each one "good." This list includes just about everything that exists. To be "good" they must not only look good but function for good as well as function smoothly together. For Paul to say "we know," he probably got this information from that chapter in Genesis. The ones called are those who fit into God's purpose. God knew something in advance about these for Paul says "for whom He foreknew, He also predestined to be conformed to the image of His Son." It was probably that they were ones that He could win back to Himself since after Adam and Eve ate of the forbidden fruit the entire human race fell into sin. It is important that God's purpose for all things working together is stated; that is, to conform them to the image of Christ. This coincides with God's statement, "Let us make man in our image." Thus, God's purpose for all creation is to have an environment for an image He is making of Himself. We can now say that Genesis 1:26 is God's **purpose statement;** therefore, our purpose for existence is to image God. The verse reads: "Then God said, 'Let Us make man in Our image, according to Our likeness; let them have dominion over the fish of the sea, over the birds of the air, and over the cattle, over all the earth and over every creeping thing that creeps on the earth.'"

When people set out to accomplish a very important task, they begin by making a clear definition of their goal, of what they intend to accomplish. This purpose statement then serves to keep them on track as well as to inform others as to what their tasks are all about. If Genesis 1:26 is truly such a statement of God's purpose for the universe in general and humans in particular, then we humans need to carefully understand each word.

In this verse, the three pronouns referring to God immediately get our attention: "us," "our," and "our." All three are plural as is the Hebrew word for God Himself, "Elohim." Though other explanations are possible for the plural forms, the only one that has biblical support is the doctrine of the Trinity. God is a corporate being, that is, three distinct persons, Father, Son, and Holy Spirit, who share one essence. They are three persons constituting one being. All three consist of exactly the same stuff. What exactly that stuff is I do not know, but since my mind thinks in terms of material things, I simply call it "spirit." What matters is that we understand that all three are equally God.

The fourth pronoun, "them," is also plural. But its antecedent is "image," a singular noun. Therefore, the image must also be a multiplicity of persons sharing the same essence. So God created Adam, a collective term for the human race as well as the personal name of the first human. He created him of two parts: first, He made the body from the dust of the ground, and second, He breathed into that body the breath of "lives," a plural in Hebrew. Together, the body and the breath constituted the first person. The creation of Eve was different, being taken from Adam, so that she was of the very same essence as Adam, that is, her body from his body and her life principle from his life principle.

Since the creation of the first couple, a multitude of people have come to planet earth. They have all appeared the same way, one cell from a male and one cell from a female uniting to form a new individual, which then has the same essence as that of Adam and Eve. All humans then equally share in the life principle possessed by Adam when he was first created. This is what makes us human and unites us all into one corporate body. The manner in which Eve was created makes this possible. This then, is one of the ways humans are truly in the image of God.

The words, "image" and "likeness" seem to be exact synonyms. A comparison of these two words in Genesis 1:26; 1:27: 5:1; 5:3; and 9:6 shows that they are interchangeable. If that is so, why then are the two words used together in the same passage? The most likely explanation is that God wants to strongly emphasize His point. He intends that this image is really going to be like Him. Since God is extremely intelligent and very capable, this image is going to be as much like God as God is able to make it. We can expect, therefore, that every attribute or characteristic of God that can be reproduced will be reproduced in the image, if not fully, then in some limited sense. Since this image will be limited by time and space as Genesis 1:1 indicates, it will not be like God in every respect. For instance, it cannot be self-existent since God is its creator. God is not limited by time or space. Thus, unlike God's ability to transcend all time, the image cannot do that as it had a beginning, but like God, it will have no end. Though God has all knowledge, His image began with none and must acquire it. Yet it seems to have an infinite capacity to do so, and at no time can anyone say that he possess all the knowledge that he or she is capable of acquiring. So, as God has all knowledge, His image has an infinite capability of learning. The image too, is confined by space, but he was given dominion over all the earth and presumably the immediate heavens that surround the earth. Then the first command that God gave him was to fill the earth, to be everywhere present on it or omnipresent.

The word "dominion" also has an important implication. Not only is man's being in the image of God, but his work also is to image God. Dominion naturally fits God, but God now permits His image to share this characteristic also. As we think of two other synonyms of this word, *control* and *power*, we can see how thoroughly it has affected every human. A person need not be very old before he clutches some item and claims ownership by using the word "mine." But God was careful to list the items over which man was permitted to exercise dominion: fish, birds, cattle, the physical earth, and over every creeping thing. The list is quite extensive and is important not only for what it includes but also for what it does not include, namely, other human beings. Jesus even explicitly forbids our dominating others (Matthew 20:25). Instead, He commands us to love, to share our very selves by submitting, giving, and serving others. Thus, we are to relate to other humans in the same way the Persons of deity relate to one another.

Man was given, to a limited degree, almost every attribute or characteristic of his Creator. In man's fallen state it is very difficult to recognize some of them. Further, some of them are not creatable and need rather to be developed, such as patience and showing mercy. The ability to develop these characteristics was given, and God continues to develop these in the lives of those currently living on planet earth. Just as patience and showing mercy must be developed, so must agape love, which is a commitment of always giving and doing the very best for others. In order to exercise agape love, a person must make a choice. It is not something God could create; people must choose to do so. Adam and Eve were given that choice when they were tested with the presence of the tree of the knowledge of good and evil in the Garden of Eden. They ate the fruit and so disobeyed God's command. To obey God and not eat of the forbidden fruit would have been the very best choice in God's universe.

I need yet to make a brief comment on the next verse following Genesis 1:26, verse 27. It is written in a different style. It is Hebrew poetry. Why? I can only speculate. Poetry is the language of the heart. As such, I think that this verse shows God's emotions. God wants us to know that after creating everything and seeing that it was "very good" He was all excited.

A word needs yet to be mentioned regarding the unity of God. It is clear that there is only **one** God, yet there are three distinct Persons, the Father, the Son, and the Holy Spirit. Each of these is referred to as God and each does the work of God. yet the Scriptures are very explicit that there is only one God. How can three be one? While speaking with the Father in John seventeen, Jesus says, "that they all may be one, as You, Father; are in Me, and I in You" (verse twenty-one). He also told Thomas that if he has seen Him, he has seen the Father.

It is very clear that they are united in one, and we accept that truth by faith.

Dare we now ask the question, "What really is God like?" Since God is in no way physical, how can we even imagine what He might look like? Is it possible? The answer is simply "no." We always think physically and when we do, we make serious mistakes. Soon after the Israelites crossed the Red Sea and Moses went up on Mt. Horeb for forty days, the people wanted a physical representation of their God. What they got was a golden calf and a severe judgment from God.

In the history of the church, various analogies have been suggested to symbolize God, especially the Trinity. An egg consisting of three parts, yolk, white, and shell, together make an egg. This analogy has the unity of God of the distinct three parts, but it must be noted that each part is made of three different materials. Water is another familiar analogy. It may exist in three different forms: a liquid, a gas, or a solid--ice. But this only illustrates a form of heresy condemned by the early church and known as modalism, that is, God changing His form from the Father to the Son, or to the Holy Spirit. In this analogy they are not different persons but rather different forms of one person.

I suggest the following diagram as an analogy of the Trinity. It shows each person as distinct by the three equal size circles. They are connected by straight parallel lines, which show equality of the same essence in each. They are connected, as well, by a wavy line, which shows inequality in their functions.

An Analogy Of God's Image

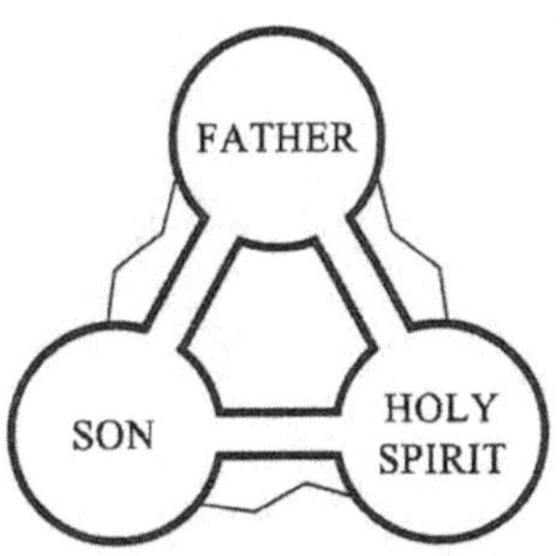

"So God created man in His own image." The very purpose for all creation is the production of this image. If the above is an accurate analogy of God, is it possible to draw a similar analogy of God's image? A circle represents Adam and a second circle represents Eve. God caused a deep sleep to come upon Adam, and then He took one of his ribs and from it created Eve. He could have taken more dust and from it created Eve, but He rather took a piece of Adam. Eve, therefore, was made of the exact same stuff or essence as Adam. A second circle of the same size as the one for Adam in our diagram represents Eve. The two parallel lines connecting them show their equality to each other. But they are not equal in every respect. Adam is appointed the leader. So a wavy line needs to be added to represent their inequality in function.

Our analogy of God's image is now very much like that for God Himself. The difference is in the number. God has three circles; man has only two. However, this is only temporary as soon children arrive in the image of the man. Where do they come from? The passage doesn't say, but they must have originated in the same fashion as all humans have since then. If so, then they came from their parents, Adam and Eve, who contributed one cell each to the making of their children.

MAN

Not good

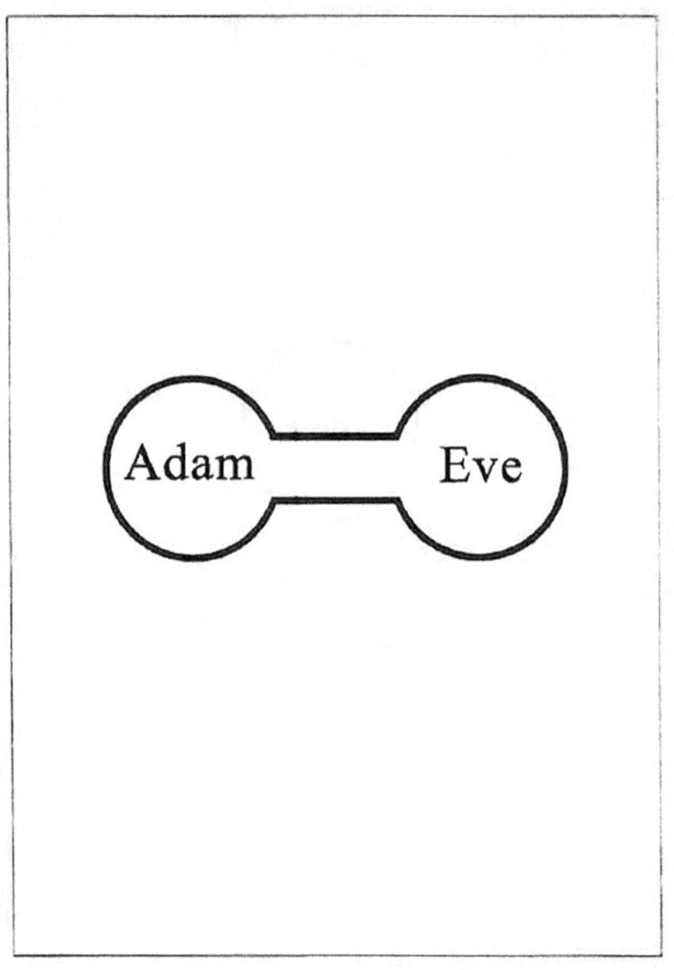

Adam
Eve

Adam
Eve

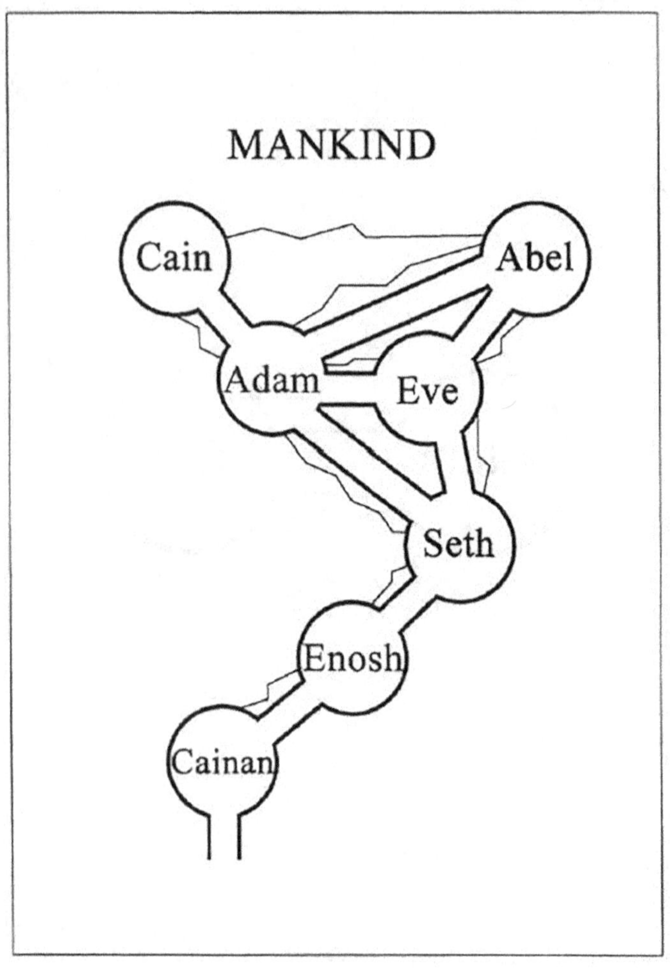

MANKIND
Cain
Abel
Adam
Eve
Seth
Enosh
Cainan

IN CHRIST

Sue
Lewis
Anna
Tim
Mary
Ken
Christ
John
Sarah
Peter
Len
Joe
Sandy

I Am

DR. JOE HUEBSCHER GREW UP as child number 11 in a family of 12 in northern Wisconsin, very much like the culture portrayed in *Little House on the Prairie.* He did not know the Lord until his family moved to Minneapolis when he was 16 years old. At that time, he quickly read through the Bible and began memorizing much of it. Following high school he entered Northwestern College, then Pillsbury College, Central Seminary, and Bob Jones University Seminary. He has taught at Maranatha Baptist Bible College and Tennessee Temple Seminary, and, in the last 25 years has spent his time traveling to and teaching in all the continents of the world.

During his years of learning and then teaching others, Dr. Huebscher has found that very few people know God's name and, of those who do, they do not really consider where He got it, why, or what it means. He has written this booklet to both help and encourage Christians to know God and His name. He trusts this booklet will further your knowledge of the One who gave His all for those who were His enemy. That is true love.